I0621492

Empire of the Dragon

Also by Pauly Hart

Empire of the Dragon

By Pauly Hart

Empire of the Dragon

Copyright © 2021 by Pauly Hart

All rights reserved. No part of this publication may be reproduced, distributed, or transmitted in any form or by any means, including photocopying, recording, or other electronic or mechanical methods, without the prior written permission of the publisher and writer, except in the case of brief quotations embodied in critical reviews and certain other noncommercial uses permitted by copyright law. For permission, requests, write to the publisher, addressed: "Attention: Permissions Coordinator," at the "Author Contact" email address below.

ISBN: 978-1-955399-04-3
Library of Congress Catalog Data is available at: Loc.gov

This book is available at cost on Amazon.com and wherever fine books are sold.

Any references to historical events, real people, or real places are used fictitiously. Names, characters, and places are products of the author's imagination.

Front cover design by Pauly Hart

Paperback version printed in Savannah, Georgia, USA, where available.

First Edition, 2021

Author Contact: EmpiresAndGenerals@gmail.com
Author Website: PaulyHart.com

For those who dream
but never wake.
For those whose slumber
nightmares make.

X Lenny

Lenny stood outside the door, a little nervous. He had heard about the man from his Druid Grove and wanted to meet him. As far as he understood, he was an ascended master of many sorts, and quite possibly, a descendant of the Tuatha Dé Danann... Which was mind-blowing. He stood outside the second floor door of the old building, nervous as hell. Everything looked super legit, but he was nervous anyway. He was an accountant and a book-keeper. This might just be his way out of the horrible jobs he'd had in the past, plus, working for a master was a once in a lifetime opportunity. He finally knocked, palms sweating.

He waited and then knocked again. Finally the door opened and a large naked man opened the door. He was on the phone and eating a pear at the same time. He waved Lenny in and then went back into the apartment, talking. Lenny stood there, not really understanding what was happening. Here was this guy, naked, talking on the phone, eating a pear? And, he... He just invited him in. It was very disorienting but Lenny worked up the nerve and came in very slowly shutting the door gently behind him.

"What? No! Not at all!" The naked man said, waving his free hand wildly in the air. "You tell him that I will eat his wife's heart for breakfast if that's what's going to happen." He slammed the phone down on the couch and Lenny could hear an animated voice still coming from the phone. The man turned to him. "Hello! You must be Leonard!" He strode over, hand extended. He was obviously unaware that he was still unclothed. At Lenny's hesitation, he appeared to have suddenly remembered.

"Oh! Excuse me!" He cried. "Let me go get some clothes on! How awful of me!" He strode away, towards the other side of the massive room, towards a wardrobe and picked out a suit for what seemed to be the longest time. He tied his long brown curly hair behind him with a loose scrunchie. The water from his hair dripped down his back, into a small puddle on the tiled floor. His toned, muscular body turned this way and that as he assembled an ensemble on the bed.

Lenny watched the whole time, not out of a sexual curiosity, only that he had never watched someone so uncaring about their nudity before. Once fully dressed, the man came back over, toweling off his hair. He had on dark black dress slacks and a dark green turtleneck. Over that, he wore a blazer the color of autumn leaves.

He watched as the man went to the kitchen area and rummage through the fridge. He brought out two clear plastic pitchers. One bright orange, the other bright red. "Would you like some?" He offered Lenny, holding up the pitchers.

"Uh, sure," Lenny croaked. "W-What is it?"

"Oh I've got orange juice and blood. I was going for a mixed drink. Maybe you want just orange juice instead?" He smiled.

"Heh. I uh, yeah." Lenny stuttered.

"Ice?" the man asked.

"Um. No." Lenny answered.

The man poured the drinks to the very rims of the cups, to where anyone would have spilled them. Placing the pitchers back in the refrigerator, he snatched the cups up and carried them over to Lenny. Lenny carefully took his, and gingerly brought it to his lips. The already condensing glass was so full it was over the top of the lip of the glass. Only the hydrostatics of the meniscus held it inside the glass, to the rest of the orange juice. He drank slowly from the top, and then tipping the glass back a little, took a slow, regular drink. It was the best orange juice he had ever tasted.

"Leonard! Not even taking the time for a toast!" The man scolded him, his own glass in his hand, not touched.

"Oops, sorry." Lenny said.

"Bah, no matter." Said the man, and brought the dark orange mixture to his lips.

"Bottoms up!" He said, and with one strange contortion, drained the whole glass into his mouth, instantly, in a free-pour. He did not seem to swallow. He smacked his lips and breathed a sigh of relief and set the glass down.

"Well?" The mas asked. "Are you going to drink yours or what?"

IX Rachel

"I just hope she's hot." Rachel texted Alice. Alice had encouraged her to reach out to the perfect match she had found on the match site. To be honest, Alice was a little bit tired of Rachel whining about her love life all the time.

"They're all dykes or lipsticks. And I want someone normal." She complained.

"You want an egg." Alice told her. "Someone you can train."

Rachel blushed at this. She wasn't a dominator but she did have a tendency to mother her lovers. "Yeah, maybe a young lipstick. But honestly, I'm still hunting that perfect Unicorn." She hunched forward on the bar table, hoping no one else was looking at her screen.

Alice didn't text back for a minute. When Rachel was going to ask her what was wrong, Alice texted: "g2g ttyl" – Rachel flipped her phone over on the table and picked up her glass. Empty. She turned around and almost hit a woman standing behind her.

"Whoa sorry!" Rachel said.

Gloria laughed. "It's ok. At least you didn't knock me over."

Rachel looked her up and down. "Hey, you looking for somebody?"

Gloria blushed. "Well yes, actually. I'm supposed to meet someone here. Are you 'Scissorblade69?'"

Rachel laughed and raised her empty glass. "Hell yeah I am! Are you "KittenFlower?"

Gloria laughed. "Yeah, caught me red-handed. Not much to hide huh?" Gloria shrugged. She was wearing a peach thigh-high skater dress and a denim jacket.

Alice would just love this one. Rachel said to herself. "I love your outfit!" is what she said out loud. "We need beer!" she held up the empty glass.

When the beer came, Gloria and Rachel got to know each other. They had similar taste in music, in sports, in women, in 18th century poets... And before you knew it, they were making out.

"Wooooooo!" One of the guys was hollering. Harry's Chocolate Shop was known as the preppy bar and usually all the Frat Rats and Sorority Swine came here, and ran off anyone else. *"Lesbians not welcome"* might as well have been stamped on their forehead.

"Let's get out of here!" Rachel shouted over the music to her, and soon, they were on the street, laughing and falling into each other.

They walked down the street a little.

"Wanna go to Triple X and get a Dwayne Purvis?" Gloria asked, a little intoxicated.

"Ewww. Peanut butter on a hamburger should be illegal." Rachel gagged.

"Fine! Wanna go to Vienna and get a coffee?" Gloria asked.

Rachel giggled. "Nope, sailor girl. Try again!"

Gloria laughed. "Fine. Want to go to my place and make out?"

Rachel laughed loudly. "Winner, winner, chicken dinner!" and shot her finger in the air.

Gloria, a little bashful, looked down with her head but up with her eyes. "You sure you wanna just go right there, right now? Don't want to know what I'm all about?"

"Come on schweety! I tawt I taw a putty tat!" Rachel laughed and tugged on her.

Gloria wasn't acting tipsy anymore. "For real though, we just met, you want to go to my place? You're sure?"

Rachel, super horny by this point, was getting a little mad at the sudden seriousness. She wanted to have fun and this frumpy little sprite was not going to ruin it.

"Look Susan..." Rachel said.

"Fuck you. It's Gloria."

"I know. I'm messing around. We might have a real connection. I just want to get you between the sheets and give you a once over." Rachel said, giving her the dreamy eyes.

Gloria couldn't help but laugh at this. "Well I'm just glad this didn't happen last week!"

Rachel squinted. "Because?"

"Aunt Flo."

Rachel laughed. "Oh! That's a relief. Mine doesn't visit for another two weeks. What are we waiting for?"

Up the newly installed elevator of the Jaques building and onto the third floor they went. When the elevator dinged, they were already halfway naked.

Rachel laughed and let her go and flung herself into the foyer.

"Oh my gaaaawd. You live here?" Rachel wheeled around, arms open. "I have been wanting to come up here since it got redone!"

Gloria gently stepped off the elevator, retrieving their clothes off the floor as she walked.

"There's a bit more to the story than you know." Gloria said. She slowly opened her purse and pulled out an American Spirit Menthol cigarette and lit it. Taking a deep breath, she studied Rachel, who stood there before her.

"Rachel." She said slowly. "Before we fuck, I want you to meet someone."

The man who wasn't there moments ago, gently placed a hand on Rachel's shoulder.

"We've been expecting you." He said, smiling.

VIII Leslie

He had seen the Jaques building construction rise, almost overnight. The top two floors matched almost identically the bottom two with the sand colored brick and the white multi-pane windows. He had watched them, because he was forced to, working behind the desk at Von's in the bookseller part. Every now and again he would miss something between customers or reshelving, and the girls at the jewelry counter would call out to him. "They're putting up more framing!"

He was curious. Ever since he had left the comic store, when Von had sold it to Jimmy John's, he itched for something else. But he and the owner, John von Erdmannsdorff, had been friends for some time. Yeah. Erdmannsdorff. That's why he just went by Von. The old man had some stones. Heck, he had survived the long lockdown, he would be just fine. Von had let most of the staff go, and it had been only four of them, all three managers and Von, who was here everyday during "The Rona" as he called it.

Leslie thanked god that he still had his job. Even though there was more footwork than the other two parts of the shop, he wouldn't trade it for his life.

Von hadn't ordered anything new, and wasn't buying any books at the moment, which drove certain townies nuts. Sure, the students would understand the transition - but the people who lived in West Lafayette (all snobs) were up in arms about their trade-in credits. Sheesh. Even though he worked in West Lafayette, he couldn't afford living in town, and lived way out on 52, almost to Montmorenci. City people were the worst. Students and actual Lafayette people were cool.

So it was with a great sigh that he helped Angie Thompson, one of his regulars. She lived up in Happy Hollow, near the Frank Lloyd Wright house, with all their zen garden feng shui crap. He would be happy when she left, but now she was furious that the books hadn't been sanitized. Her name should really be "Karen."

"I want to speak to Von! Tell him I'm here and I want these book sanitized!" She yelled, muffled through her double mask.

"Ma'am there's really..." He started.

"Don't you 'Ma'am' me mister! At least you should provide gloves so I can look at each individual book without contamination! And I'll need a new pair of gloves for each book I want to look at!" She yelled again.

He wondered how she could even get enough oxygen to do all that yelling without passing out.

He had a mask on too, just for aesthetics, but it didn't help. He'd read the research on Carbon Dioxide buildup. He didn't wear it when people weren't in the store.

Eventually Mrs. Thompson left and he was alone again. She'd huffed and puffed her way through the books, not touching anything, warning him that she'd be back.

"Don't let the door hit you on your way out." He mumbled, after she left.

He shelved books for a while and there were no customers. He called to Adrienne, the jewelry, beads, and rocks manager. "Headed out for a smoke!"

"Okay!" She called back, from up the stairs.

He stepped out in front. Since they were so low on employees, he really didn't have a chance to grab a full smoke.

Standing in front of the building, he pulled out an American Spirit Menthol, pulled his mask down, and lit it - staring at the building across the street. They had just finished the fourth and fifth floors? Wait... One – Convenience store... Two – Old Dance Studio... Three? Three was missing maybe. It was all façade? Interesting. Maybe those were the third and fourth floors? But no, because of the spacing it had to be four and five. They were only zoned for four floors.

It didn't make any sense. Because the height was off. It was like one of those hotels with a missing 13th floor, not even listed on the elevator. But then there's some horror story about how there really is a 13th floor and you can get all sorts of spooky tales and stuff from that. Damn, he loved a good story. Someone honked.

He looked at the passing car, didn't recognize them, but waved anyway. A friendly gesture. And then it happened. Like, when a low flying airplane appears out of nowhere that you didn't hear and the sun catches it and then you suddenly hear it? Something like that happened right as he waved. At the very moment he was putting his arm down, some kind of light and loud boom went right through him and it scared the shit out of him. He dropped his cigarette and looked around. Nothing.

What? Like a ripple in water, it washed over him and things were different. He couldn't explain it... Just different. He looked up at the building across the street. Four floors. One, two... Three, four. Just like they planned it. But Waitaminute. There were five floors. Weren't there? Leslie scratched his head. That was really weird. There were five floors. There had to have been. Because the third floor façade was too tall. It was five.

Then he saw the man on the fourth floor, what was the fifth, until the ripple. He was holding up four fingers looking straight at Leslie.

IV Damien

It was another dull night. Damien was at The Tap, out on the patio, watching the game. The cars were driving by shouting their Boilermaker Pride at the top of their lungs. The girls' volleyball team had won again. It wasn't the same atmosphere as when the men's football team won, but then again, people like Drew Brees only came around once in a lifetime. His fraternity sponsor used to go to Drew's parties all the time in downtown Lafayette, just across the bridge and told him wild stories. Wow. What a time to have been here at school.

Another sip, another failed IPA. "I swear these guys just don't know what they're doing." He murmured to himself and took another sip.

"Hey buddy!" Came the call of the man, the legend, the machine. It was Nick. Good old Saint Nick, rich bastard and loved to show it. "Barkeep!" He howled at a server walking by. "Another pitcher of whatever this is!"

"Oh no, actually..." Damien started, but she had already gone.

Nick plonked down beside him and put his arm over his shoulder. "Ah Damien, my old friend, how fares the night?" He smiled and pulled out an American Spirit Menthol cigarette. He loved looking the part.

"Oh, okay I guess." Damien thought. *Until you sat down,* he added in his head. Nick was a, hmm. What was the right word? A boor? Yeah. Probably right. Nick's parents had all the money but had never taught Nick to use it well. He's probably waste all his parents money and die alone and in poverty. What a swell guy. But he did have the hookups. Everyone knew *about* Nick, but Nick treated everyone like shit. Not Damien for some reason. Probably because Damien had never called Nick out on his bullcrap. He may never. He saw good in Nick. Just a little.

"You think any more about investing in my dad's company?" Damien said, eyeballing him over the cigarette. "I know you could make a lot of money.

Damien shrugged. "Don't really have any money to invest man. I told you. I'm broke as a joke. I can't even afford this next pitcher coming. You going to get it?"

Nick laughed his *richer than the peasants* laugh. "Ah dear boy! Never fear! Jolly old Saint Nick is here to spread the cheer!" Then pounded the table like he had just come up with the whole thing, on the fly... Truth is, when Nick got a little liquor in him, he said it every time but then always argued about the bill with the server.

Just then the server came back with the pitcher and asked "Start a tab?"

Nick smiled at her and handed her a twenty.

"Change?" She asked.

"Nah. Thanks babe." He said and smiled.

"Sure." She said frowning, and went back inside.

"Wow you're feeling generous tonight," Damien said. "A whole two dollar tip!"

"Who are you and what have you done with my friend?" Nick asked. "Of course I'm generous! I'm Saint Nick!" He took a drink. "Woah. But right now, jolly old Saint Nick has to pee!" He hopped up and went back inside, leaving Damien caught in the turbulence of the situation.

"Ugh." Damien said, and poured himself a drink from the fresh pitcher.

A little while later, after drinking two more glasses, Damien realized he'd been stood up. *Stupid Nick. Buying me crap beer then disappearing.* He turned around and sat in his seat to where he could see everyone else. *All alone again on a Friday. Same old story.* He was done. He was tired and a little drunk and was tired of waiting.

He got up and... *Woah... Ok.* He got up again, this time using the patio table to steady him. *Make it to the door. Check.* The mental list was going to be short and good. A series of small successes would get him back to the apartment where he could pass out in peace.

Through the bar. Check.

Wave goodbye. Check.

Out the front. Check.

Don't step into traffic. Check.

Up the block. Check.

Turn right on the alley. Check.

Don't bump into that guy. Che-.

"Oops sorry man." Damien said. He had bumped into that guy. That was bad. Maybe the guy would leave him alone... Nope.

Damien hit the brick wall hard and had the wind knocked out of him.

"Watch where you're going meat." The man said.

Woah, this dude was strong.

"I – I said I'm sorry." Damien stammered.

"How about I punch you and then call it even?" The big man said with a hard smile.

"W-what?" Damien asked, in disbelief.

The big man let him go and Damien leaned against the brick wall, where the man had pushed him.

"No biggie kid." The man said. "I'll just punch you once, on the nose for bumping into me, then we'll call it even."

"That's not even fair –" Damien said.

"Ready, here it comes!" The man said, and took a really big swing at him.

Reflexes took over and Damien jerked his head back before the fist hit him.

Wham, the back of his head hit the brick wall and hurt like a sonofabitch.

"Ow! Damien cried and jerked his head away. It took him a little bit, but realized the man hadn't punched him at all – he stopped the punch before it hit him, knowing exactly what Damien would do.

"Ah, ha ha ha," the man laughed hard. "That's a classic," and continued laughing.

After a moment the man came back to himself. "Now get out of here, before rip your throat out and tie it around your neck."

Damien ran the rest of the way home.

He didn't notice the unmarked police car idling on the curb.

VII Gloria

"Gloria, this is Leonard, my aide. He and I will both be interviewing you for the job, so don't be afraid. Be calm, and answer honestly." The very handsome man in the white suit said, as he leaned back in his chair. Leonard, his aide, was younger and not as good looking, but his slicked back hair and business attire made him look powerful. She was so nervous she almost peed a little.

"Alright. Sounds good." Gloria said. Sitting up in her seat.

"OK Gloria," Leonard began, "What we're looking for is an assistant to the boss, Doctor Jeff here, to be with him daily. Filling his schedule, answering his calls, collating and answering emails, and preparing communications. Is this something you feel you'd be capable of doing?"

"Oh yes, definitely. My last job I was a TA at Purdue. It's a lot of the same thing." Gloria said, confidently.

"What department?" Jeff asked.

"Division of Military Science and Technology at Purdue Polytechnic - at Lafayette." She smiled.

"That's over at the Subaru Plant?" Jeff asked.

"Yes. We worked with Japanese Robotics primarily and their applications in the real world battlefield scenario." Gloria said.

"Mmm." Jeff said, steepling his fingers. "I see."

Leonard took over. "And what were your responsibilities there?"

"Um, daily transitions of work orders disseminating from the Japanese engineers to the floor among the Group and Team leaders of Subaru employees. We also handled data transfer. For instance with the release of the Ascent, there were only certain employees who would work on it. They've transferred that to Polytechnic with the newest model."

"Which is?" Jeff asked.

"Um. I'm still under NDA and can't discuss." Gloria said, a little bashfully.

Jeff, who had been leaning back in his chair, now came forward and put his elbows on the table.

"Glooooooria." He said, syrupy. "If we're to work together, we have to trust each other."

"Well I understand that, but I really..."

He cut her off. "Gloooooooriaaaaaa. Come now." He put out his hand across the table, offering it to her.

She was a little shaken, but tentatively put her hand out and touched his.

Grabbing it, he held it gently but firmly, like a boa constrictor. He smiled very broadly.

"Gloriaaaaaaa." He said again, and this time, she felt her mind melt away.

Someone clapping. Clapping. When would they shut up with the clapping? Gloria? Gloria? Hello? Gloria? Fingers snapping. Someone shaking her. Huh?

She opened her eyes slowly, as if she'd been a bear in hibernation. Woah. She was in the office. Jeff and that Leonard guy were hovering above her.

"Gloria!" Jeff shouted. "Are you alright?" He asked, and brought her to sit upright. She was on the floor. She wiped her lip. She was drooling. She looked around. Why was she on the floor? What?

"Let me help you up." Jeff said. He picked her light frame up with ease and helped her stand. "Would you like some water?" He said. "Leonard, get water." Leonard left the room and around the corner.

"Let's sit you down." He brought her over to the chair, a little tightly. The underwire from her bra poked the other side a little. That was tight. He set her down in the chair and then squatted down so they were eye to eye. "You alright there kid? You gave us quite a scare." He looked deeply into her eyes, and she felt a bit foggy again.

"Uhhh. Ya. I'm alright. I just – just need to sit here for a minute."

Leonard returned with the water and she drank some. Leonard picked up the papers that had fallen on the floor. Jeff remained standing.

Gloria was quite embarrassed and you could hear it in her voice. When she was stressed, her South African accent came back. "How long was I out?" She asked. She looked at her phone. It was later than she thought. How long was she out?"

Leonard looked at Jeff, who stood looking down at her.

"Gloria. You did give us quite a scare. I'm afraid that Leonard and I will have to go over this new information about your health and take it into consideration." He was through being concerned over her. Now he was impatient.

He stepped to the glass door and held it.

"We will be in touch." He said.

VI Vik

Vik Patel wrestled with the inner security door until he finally got it closed. His wife had asked the building owner time and time again to please fix the problem but he hadn't gotten back to her. He was a pleasant enough man to talk to. He came in the other day to buy a pack of Natural Spirits, something he had never done before.

"I tasted them the other day, now I'm just curious to what they taste like." The owner had told him. Such an odd thing to say. How could he taste them if he had never tasted them? Maybe it was an American thing. He still was trying to get the Michael Jackson "bad equals good" thing down, which his wife told him he might never do, so just give up.

He had been here all day working. Working hard was not the problem, it was just that it continued on and on. There didn't seem to be an end in sight. All of his boys were too young to work the store. His oldest, Ramesh would sometimes sweep and mop. He only had Ramesh help if he had done poorly in school. So it was a discipline. That wasn't really fair to the boy, but Vik wanted him to become a doctor, not inherit the store.

He was torn between being a good Hindu man and a good husband. On one foot, he knew that none of this mattered and that eventually karma would reincarnate him as something wiser and better than this life. He was a good Hindu and dwelt in this land at the behest of his dutiful wife. He wanted to be good to her. Yet karma also told him that none of it mattered. He would always come back as something else. So he should enjoy the fruits of his labors now and not wait.

Oh what a lousy disciple of truth he was. Seeking fleeting pleasures and not adhering to his word. He had married the wonderful woman and moved to the United States thinking that everything was possible... That's before he realized how expensive children were. They changed everything. With every son his wife bore, he became poorer and poorer. If they had never brought any other souls to life, they might be well off one day, maybe the owners of this building... But no. They had four money-eaters and it was too much.

He finally got the gate shut and stepped back in. Once the register had been counted and the credit card batch settled, he zipped it all up into the blue bank bag and tucked it under his arm. He would go home, drink a beer, help the children with homework, and maybe his wife would let him get lucky.

As he neared the back of the shop, he noticed a very bad smell. Oh no. He walked to the milk cooler. There it was, an entire gallon of milk spilled all over the floor. Seriously though? Vik could not believe his eyes. He'd had customers all day and none of them told him about the mess? To be fair, the milk cooler was tucked away in the corner by itself, and not many people had come to use it yet. But it was a standalone unit and there was no room anywhere else for it. On recollection, he honestly couldn't recall selling anything from the cooler all day. This is why no one told him. But it appeared almost a whole day old, and smelled even worse. Maybe the college kids expected that. Maybe they thought his convenience store was supposed to smell that way. This made him even a little more sad.

He put the bank bag down and went around the back of the cooler. Yes. The milk had gone all the way down the back wall and gotten under everything. Empty cartons and Pepsi totes were standing in rotten milk. What a great way to end this very bad day.

His son had been the last one to use the mop. It was in the basement at the foot of the stairwell. He went down to get it. Sopping wet and not cleaned from the last mop, it stank too. He sighed while he cleaned the mop and filled the bucket to clean to milk. Lugging the full bucket up the stairs, he sighed again and started to clean. Thirty minutes later, he finally finished and lugged the bucket back down the stairs, dumped it, cleaned the mop, and hung it to dry. This was when he heard the steady dropping of liquid.

Drip, drip, drip went the sound. He walked down the hallway to have a better look. If milk had gotten into the floor and was dripping down here, he would have to pay for it. The best thing to do was to clean it before the owner found out.

The basement was full of locked doors, some with old fittings, from the 1940's and some newer. The dripping was coming from behind the newest door. He grabbed the handle. It wasn't locked. Turning the lock he opened the door and saw the most miraculous thing he had ever seen.

On the floor, on pallets, were large gold bars. More gold than he had ever seen in his life or on TV. He was so transfixed with the vision that he didn't notice the man behind him.

Schnort! Vik said as he jerked his head up from the counter. He must have fallen asleep at the counter. He had cleaned up the milk and put the mop away... And then... And then he must have come up here to put his head down for a minute.

Odd. I don't remember taking a nap. He thought. *I really should be heading home. Oh, I have a headache. Maybe the best thing for me to do is to go straight to bed.*

He walked out the back door and to his car, rubbing the base of his neck all the way.

II McGuffin

It was a starry night on Chauncey Hill and Mac sat on the top of the Jaques building lost in thought. He'd smoked his last bong and didn't know where else to score. Broncey wasn't holding and Claire was out of town, and he didn't have any money. He'd heard that the new owner of the building was coming into town today but he hadn't left his spot yet. Maybe he would let him stay up here, away from the world. Down on the street he could hear the music from all the bars and shops. Where Else was jamming some hip hop. It used to be a techno club, back in the day. Now it was just a spot to get drunk and grind. Jakes had a band out on the patio. That was pretty cool. Usually they were inside. Some mellow Grateful Dead stuff. Wild.

The cars that went by were all the same. One in a hundred went *THOOM THOOM* with the crank of oversized bass cabinets attached with chicken wire to their 1985 Lincoln Town Cars. Knuckleheads. They think they're rich, Mac mused. He lit an American Spirits Menthol from his stash. Getting low on smokes too. He needed money, but didn't know where to get it. Cops around The Village were all the same, and they all knew him. He couldn't hustle on the street. The only thing to do was some dumpster diving. He probably could score some street butts too, or maybe some booze... But he was too smelly for any real work. He needed a shower but the water on the top floor of the building had been turned off, so he couldn't even do that.

Maybe Susan would let me come in her apartment again? Maybe. Probably not. She was fucking someone else now, some tall girl from India. Oh well. He didn't swing both ways, but if Susan was nice, maybe they would be up for a threesome. Maybe. It was time to get down.

He crept out from under the tarp and looked up to the Mad Mushroom building. Nobody on their roof tonight. He looked towards the Target building. No one there either. He peeked over the front, real low. No one could see him and Von's was already closed. So that was cool. He could go out from the hatch or back the fire escape. Hatch would be safer, but he didn't know about the new owner yet. If he was in then he would be caught. Waitaminute. That was stupid. People who owned buildings didn't visit in the night, unless there was a fire or something, and maybe not even then. It would be alright.

He opened the hatch real slowly, anyway. No use in making noise. Climbing down to the top floor was slow going, because the metal ladder was a bit crumbly, but he made it. It was dark, obviously. But there was stuff unpacked here and there. They must have come while he was sleeping. Wow. That was lucky they hadn't seen him. Mac made a note to get all his stuff and scram after his foraging tonight, before morning came. He just needed to score a place to be before all that. And he didn't have any ideas yet.

Wow. There was some weird stuff here. Huge stone blocks? What was that? Why did they bring up stone? Were they redoing something? But with stone? Mac couldn't figure it. Then one of the stone blocks moved. What?

The top slid off of it and there was a huge thud on the floor. Crap. What in the world was...

Before Mac could make sense of it, a dark figure rose from the block, and Mac realized it must be a sarcoff... A Sarcofoh... One of those mummy things. Damn. That dude was just standing there, eyes shut... Wait. The eyes opened and all Mac saw in the dark were two glowing eyes, bright red. Demon red. Death red.

That was the last thing Mac ever saw.

III Saanvi

Vikramaditya Ramish Patel owned his own business back in Champagne, Illinois. He had liked it there but the whole state was going down the tubes. One day when his wife was exploring Craigslist, she stumbled upon the Jaques building rental. It was only $1,500 per month and she knew they could make it there. Saanvi called her dearest husband on the phone.

"Vik, I know what you are thinking but you need to listen to this." And she told him about it. He was the poor husband who worked at the store and let her make all the decisions. So it was, about a month later, they broke their crappy lease and made the move. Sure, they lost their deposit of $2,000 but it was worth it. $4,500 at that location was steep and they only netted double that. In Indiana they could triple or quadruple that easily. College students needed cigarettes and fountain drinks.

The move went fairly easily. When they arrived the former owners of the print shop were finishing their demolition and it was the second of the month. The building owner was nowhere to be found and the print shop people wouldn't even let them in. Even though their deposit had gone through and they were supposed to be getting keys that day. She called him on the phone, furious.

"Mister Jeff! They are telling me that I cannot come in and I am very unhappy about this! You had best give me a pro-rate on my rent!" She scolded him in her typical high-pitched scolding voice that she usually reserved for her husband or four sons. They were a handful, so she really knew how to get under their skin.

"Woah there biscuit-cakes. We'll figure it out," Jeff said, nonplussed. He was busy working out some toe-jam from between his toes, rubbing them a little too raw. "If all sits well with the print shop guys, we can have you in there... Say, Thursday?" It was Tuesday today, so he added: "Look, and I'll give you half month's rent, so you can relax. $750 should be enough, right?"

She didn't usually fall for that kind of thing, but there was something in his voice that moved her to obey. Something dark. She couldn't place it... But didn't want to argue. "Uh, ok then Mister Jeff. That's fine. Yes, we can do that. I just want you to know that I am very motivated to move in." She hung up the phone, shaking.

He smiled and said: "Fine. See you Thursday morning," and clicked the call off. One day should give him enough time to cover the windows and perform some incantations. He would need his regulars and a couple of willing kid sacrifices. Not goats this time, he smiled, but children. Maybe one of hers.

X Sophia

The Duct tape covering Sophia's mouth had begun to come undone. She was working the bottom of it with her tongue a little here and there because she thought she was finally alone. She was brave for a twelve year old but the blindfold still itched. The floor was cold and it smelled like the halls of school. Bleach, she thought. Her shoulders hurt too, they tied her elbows and wrists together.

There were people singing or something in the other room. All she could do is think about that creepy time at her friend's house during Halloween. That time her friend's dad wanted to touch her but she went home instead. She never told anybody. She never told Ashley. Was this Ashley's house? She didn't think so. She doesn't remember a metal floor. That's what it felt like. A whole floor of metal. She also needed to pee.

The door opened and the singing was suddenly all around her. Just then, she finished getting her mouth to open and screamed loud. I mean, super loud.

"Help! Somebody He..." But she never got passed that because someone slapped her so hard, she didn't need to pee anymore. A dark spot formed on her jeans and a man's voice said: "Goddammit. You little shit." She didn't try to say anything else, but they got the duct tape and wound it around her head around her mouth three times, getting her hair in it. It wasn't like the movie's duct tape.

They took off the blindfold and she could finally see a little, but it was upside down because they were carrying her on a pole. When they brought her to a large stone block, they hung her on "x" poles next to it and formed a big circle. Everyone was dressed in big creepy brown robes and chanting. They held hands and chanted something for a while in another language, then four men went over to the block and took the lid off and Sophia peed again.

Up from the bottom of the cube was a black figure. Black and green with red glowing eyes. He stepped out and Sophia saw his tail whipping back and forth, long and green. He was naked and there was something else that wasn't his tail in front of him.

They put the stone back on the block, picked her up and put her on top of it. They undid the tape around her arms and locked her down on the top of it. Then they got scissors out and cut off all her clothes. The large black shape walked around and around her and the people in robes sung a weird song.

When they were done singing, the black shape raised his hands and yelled something really bizarre and then crawled on top of her.

When the door burst in it was loud. "Police!" A woman's voice called. "Get down on the ground and spread your hands!"

Everyone started yelling at once and then one of the men in the robes raised a shotgun. Suddenly, the dark room was bright with gunfire. When it was all over, Detective Velasquez kicked several guns away from the dead bodies.

"All of them in robes. Where's the big green guy?" She asked.

There was no way in or out, and he was not there.

"Anyone hurt? Sound off!" She called.

"We're alright Detective!" Said the lead man.

"Good, let's check on the girl."

"Then they brought me here." Sophia said to the woman on the couch. Her eyes, vacant, searching the floor. She didn't offer any more.

"And that's all you remember?" The woman tapped her pencil on the notebook. "What happened to the dark shape? What happened to Gloria?"

"I don't know. I told you everything. I even told you I wet myself ok? What do you want?"

"Nothing more for now sweetie," the woman said, closing her notebook and setting it down on the end-table, next to her American Spirit Menthols. "We're done, ok? You're safe. It's over."

"Ok," Sophia said, looking down at the ground.

In the background, the wall clock gave a faint *tic, tic, tic.*

I Jeff

Dragon magic only works if the user is sitting on top of cursed gold, has the right hexes drawn, and is in fact, a dragon. Jeff woke up one day with a particular day with a strong desire to eat a virgin. There was particular reason for this; they just tasted better than regular folk. Virginity was a delicacy of sorts... A lost flavor in this modern day and age. Like most dragons of his kind, he could smell it on people, especially women.

Virginity smelled like fresh plums to him. No matter the gender of the person, it was a ripe and pungent smell - an olfactory delight. But he was in a minority of dragons. He would rather eat them than deflower them... Regardless of gender. His quest was the pallet, and not the spoiling of the fruit.

Jeff wasn't a full dragon, so this modified his tastes somewhat. His father, a full dragon, had given him most of his ferocity - but it was from his mother's side where he had developed many of his quirks. Jeff's mother's father was a Preta, and his grandmother was a Seraph. The rape had spawned his mother, and his father had taken her as a blood-oath to The Order.

That's The Presiding Order of The Fraternal Order of Architects, today. When his father was around, they had a similar name. In today's litigious lifestyle, the names were shuffled around in shell corporations here and there in many a small Caribbean country. Jeff thinks that this last one was Cayman or something like that. Who really knew besides the elders? And Jeff was on the outs with them at the moment.

A lot of his problem with The Order had to do with his established heritage. His grandfather, the Preta, wasn't really around anymore to prove his legitimacy. His grandmother, appealed to them, showing the birth records from the coven she had birthed his mother. The Order did not recognize The Covens papers. They said that true vampirism could never be proven. It was a circus court and the whole thing had drove Jeff to leave The Order and seek his fortune on his own, and not in blessed France. The old Merovingian Masters would do just fine without him. He would go to America to seek his fortune. He had mastered the Ohio Valley dialect with ease. Most of the actors on TV spoke it anyway. It would be a breeze. He would start his own Order. Damn them all to Hades.

Things were looking brighter already. He had just procured a parcel off Chauncey Hill, where Jakes Pizza had set up shop for years. Right before you got to Von's off Northwestern and State Street. If you've ever visited West Lafayette or Purdue University, you know exactly where Amused Clothing used to be. That was where he was. Amused had finally gone under. Shame really, they had some cool stuff.

They've done a lot of work in that area. The corner building next to "Where Else?" dance club was now a Target Store and apartments, and the Chauncey Hill Village Mall where folks used to get their "Den Pop" at Discount Den was gone. The den had been there for 37 years, so it was a good run. The whole area was undergoing renovation. His building, though, not on the actual corner, was still going to be worth millions. He just had to HODL. That was one of the only words he had learned in cryptocurrency investing. "Hold On for Dear Life" - and it was one of the more powerful ones. Investing for the long term was one of his greatest attributes.

He would probably never sell the building. The Jaques building was formerly owned by a little old lady from upstate New York, and he'd wheeled and dealed her until the sale went through. There may or may not have been some blood magic used. Jeff would deny anything like that... But yes, there had been a lot of energy manipulation to get that to push through. She was stubborn, but now, she was dead and the building was his.

Now that Jeff was the owner, he could do what he wanted. The old dance studio that was on the third floor was a perfect space for his new business front. Wonderful. He could look down at the wanton sheep on Friday nights and have his fill. Most Purdue students lost their virginity their freshman year. The college was an agricultural college for the most part, but they did have some engineering and art students. He liked art engineering the best. Sex to most of them was something of a mystery, but he was a humble soul, and he would train them... And if not sex, per se, then unexpected death... Or kidnapping... Or just violation. Those were fun too.

Jeff didn't like the Christian girls. Or the Jewish ones. There weren't much of either, but there were some. Back when Tom's donuts and Pete's bar were in full swing, there had been more, but the whole culture had dipped downwards. That was both good and bad. Culturally, it was fun to watch the demise of such a normal place as the Heartland of middle Indiana take a nose-dive... But for culinary delights, finding virgins became more of a hassle.

The good news is - most of them didn't consider sodomy to be sex. Or oral. Sex to them was actual penetration. Jeff knew better. Those soul ties were something of a mystery to the average college student - or anyone for that matter. He knew what was sex. It was more than penetration. It was a matter of the soul binding to another; this was at the core of any magic anyway. Jeff had bound himself to more souls than most, and it gave him more energy.

That was the thing: Energy. And he had plenty of sources to choose from. The whole of the town would tremble before him. Eventually when he controlled West Lafayette and Purdue, he would control the other side of the River, into Lafayette itself. He already had the old Great Lakes Chemical building land in sight. He just hoped he could get there before developers snatched it up. And then there was downtown. He wanted the Java Roaster building, and several others around the courthouse. He would have to be patient.

Ah, plans... How they evolve. He wanted everything... But he would start with this small town in Indiana.

Nulla Alexi

Alexi knew the Ruach Ho'kodesh was alive and well in his heart. He had just gotten saved. Since leaving the Russian Orthodox Church he had been on a direct collision course with love and happiness. The more he poured over the Odiot Paleo-Hebrew language, the more he understood all the things that his church had not told him. Learning Torah directly from the scriptures had been one of the largest growth experiences of his life. HIs family wasn't pleased about his new American traditions. His family wasn't pleased about anything not rooted in Mother Russia anyway, so that was expected.

He'd come to Purdue to study engineering. He was a huge fan of Neal Armstrong and the NASA program. But the more he fell in love with The Word of the Old Testament, the more he fell out of love with NASA. One of the largest "Mind-bombs" that hit him was finding out "Nasha" meant to deceive. Their name meant deception? What else could it be but The Ruach pulling him away from his old loves and into his new one.

When Alexi first saw the man on the sidewalk looking up at the old dance studio, his heart froze. This was the man from his dream three nights ago. In his dream the man rose on large leather wings. He stopped walking to observe him on the street. The man stood looking at the large building chanting something, fingers playing against each other, in an odd, waving way. Something was not right with him. Not right at all.

He prayed then and there for wisdom in what to do and instantly he remembered the nice policeman he talked to several weeks ago. He thought he still had his card in his phone case... Yes. Here it was. He would give him a call and find out if there was something to be done.

He dialed. The phone rang and a woman picked up.

"Velasquez." The voice said.

He told her who he was and about the man.

"There's nothing wrong with standing and looking at a building sir. Unless this is an emergency, and it doesn't appear that it is, then you need to hang up and dial 9-1-1." She said flatly.
He asked her if she believed in God.

She said she did.

"Then listen well to what I am telling you Mrs. Police lady. There is a God and His name is Yahweh and he gives his children guidance form the inside, through the precious Holy Spirit. He is guiding me to call you because I had an evil dream about a man, and now he is standing before me. I don't know what led me to walk along Northwestern, but here I am and now I have been led to call you. Do with this information what you will, but I am only a servant in obedience."

There was a long pause.

"Sir. I do recall you now, and as I recall, you're from Russia and you had parked illegally. I let you off with a warning that day. Maybe there is something to what you're saying, and maybe there's not, but I can't deny the gut feeling that I need to really pay this matter some attention. Now, describe the man you're looking at, and tell me honestly what you think is going on."

He did, and she paid attention.

www.ingramcontent.com/pod-product-compliance
Lightning Source LLC
Chambersburg PA
CBHW021006150626
46549CB00012BA/1370